Put Beginning Readers on the Right Track with
ALL ABOARD READING™

The All Aboard Reading series is especially designed for beginning readers. Written by noted authors and illustrated in full color, these are books that children really want to read—books to excite their imagination, expand their interests, make them laugh, and support their feelings. With fiction and nonfiction stories that are high interest and curriculum-related, All Aboard Reading books offer something for every young reader. And with four different reading levels, the All Aboard Reading series lets you choose which books are most appropriate for your children and their growing abilities.

Picture Readers
Picture Readers have super-simple texts, with many nouns appearing as rebus pictures. At the end of each book are 24 flash cards—on one side is a rebus picture; on the other side is the written-out word.

Station Stop 1
Station Stop 1 books are best for children who have just begun to read. Simple words and big type make these early reading experiences more comfortable. Picture clues help children to figure out the words on the page. Lots of repetition throughout the text helps children to predict the next word or phrase—an essential step in developing word recognition.

Station Stop 2
Station Stop 2 books are written specifically for children who are reading with help. Short sentences make it easier for early readers to understand what they are reading. Simple plots and simple dialogue help children with reading comprehension.

Station Stop 3
Station Stop 3 books are perfect for children who are reading alone. With longer text and harder words, these books appeal to children who have mastered basic reading skills. More complex stories captivate children who are ready for more challenging books.

In addition to All Aboard Reading books, look for All Aboard Math Readers™ (fiction stories that teach math concepts children are learning in school); All Aboard Science Readers™ (nonfiction books that explore the most fascinating science topics in age-appropriate language); All Aboard Poetry Readers™ (funny, rhyming poems for readers of all levels); and All Aboard Mystery Readers™ (puzzling tales where children piece together evidence with the characters).

All Aboard for happy reading!

For our little "polar bears," Imani, Jeffrey, Lema,
Tay-tay, Joseph, and Isabella.—P.J.

GROSSET & DUNLAP
Published by the Penguin Group
Penguin Group (USA) Inc., 375 Hudson Street,
New York, New York 10014, USA
Penguin Group (Canada), 90 Eglinton Avenue East, Suite 700,
Toronto, Ontario M4P 2Y3, Canada
(a division of Pearson Penguin Canada Inc.)
Penguin Books Ltd., 80 Strand, London WC2R 0RL, England
Penguin Group Ireland, 25 St. Stephen's Green, Dublin 2, Ireland
(a division of Penguin Books Ltd.)
Penguin Group (Australia), 250 Camberwell Road, Camberwell, Victoria 3124, Australia
(a division of Pearson Australia Group Pty. Ltd.)
Penguin Books India Pvt. Ltd., 11 Community Centre, Panchsheel Park,
New Delhi—110 017, India
Penguin Group (NZ), 67 Apollo Drive, Rosedale, North Shore 0632, New Zealand
(a division of Pearson New Zealand Ltd.)
Penguin Books (South Africa) (Pty.) Ltd., 24 Sturdee Avenue,
Rosebank, Johannesburg 2196, South Africa

Penguin Books Ltd., Registered Offices: 80 Strand, London WC2R 0RL, England

Text copyright © 2008 by Roberta Edwards. Illustrations copyright © 2008 by Pamela
Johnson. All rights reserved. Published by Grosset & Dunlap, a division of Penguin Young
Readers Group, 345 Hudson Street, New York, New York 10014.
ALL ABOARD SCIENCE READER and GROSSET & DUNLAP are trademarks of
Penguin Group (USA) Inc. Printed in the U.S.A.

Library of Congress Cataloging-in-Publication Data

Edwards, Roberta.
Polar bears : in danger / by Roberta Edwards ; illustrated by Pamela Johnson.
p. cm. -- (All aboard science reader. Station stop 2)
ISBN-13: 978-0-448-44924-1 (pbk.)
1. Polar bear--Juvenile literature. 2. Endangered species--Juvenile literature. I. Johnson,
Pamela, ill. II. Title.
QL737.C27E35 2008
599.786--dc22
2007046911

ISBN 978-0-448-44924-1   10 9 8 7 6 5 4 3 2

POLAR BEARS
IN DANGER

By Roberta Edwards
Illustrated by Pamela Johnson

Grosset & Dunlap

At the top of the world

near the North Pole

lies the Arctic Ocean.

A thick layer of ice floats

on its surface.

It is bitter cold here.

The winds are fierce.

In winter it is dark out

nearly all day long.

This is where polar bears

make their home.

A male polar bear stands

near a hole in the ice.

He watches and waits.

What is the bear waiting for?

He knows a seal is below.

Ringed seals are his favorite food.

Sooner or later

the seal must come up for air.

When it does,

the polar bear lunges.

One punch knocks

out the seal.

The polar bear feasts on the dead seal.

This is as much meat as is in

four hundred hamburgers!

After a big meal,

the polar bear can go several days

before eating again.

Polar bears are the largest
meat-eaters on land.
Some weigh as much as 1,700 pounds
and are eleven feet tall standing up.

That's as tall as an elephant.

Do you think polar bears
are white?

If you do, you're wrong.

Their fur has no color.

Light reflecting off their fur
makes it look white.

Under the fur

their skin is black.

Black holds in more heat

than any other color.

Having black skin

helps polar bears stay warm.

So does a thick layer of fat—

it's like extra padding!

The layer of fat also

makes it easy for polar bears to float.

Unlike other bears,

polar bears spend

a lot of time in the water.

They swim from one big chunk
of ice to the next.
They can go for
sixty miles without stopping.
They can stay underwater
for two minutes.

Young polar bears

learn to swim and hunt

by watching their mother.

A mother polar bear usually

gives birth to two cubs

at a time.

At birth, the cubs
are tiny—no bigger than rats!
They can't see at all.

They are born in a den

deep inside the snow.

The cubs stay here

for several months.

All this time

the mother does not eat.

She lives off the fat stored

in her body.

The mother cuddles her cubs
to keep them warm.
She feeds them with her milk.

By early spring

the cubs are the size

of small dogs.

They are ready to leave the den.

The mother is ready for

her first meal in five months!

The cubs follow

their mother out of the den.

A male polar bear or an Arctic wolf

might attack her babies.

So the mother steps outside first.

She makes sure

there is no danger.

Right away,

the cubs are ready

to play in the snow.

They slide down hills.

They roll and tumble

with their mother.

Then the mother and her cubs
walk to the coast.
There, she will hunt for seals.

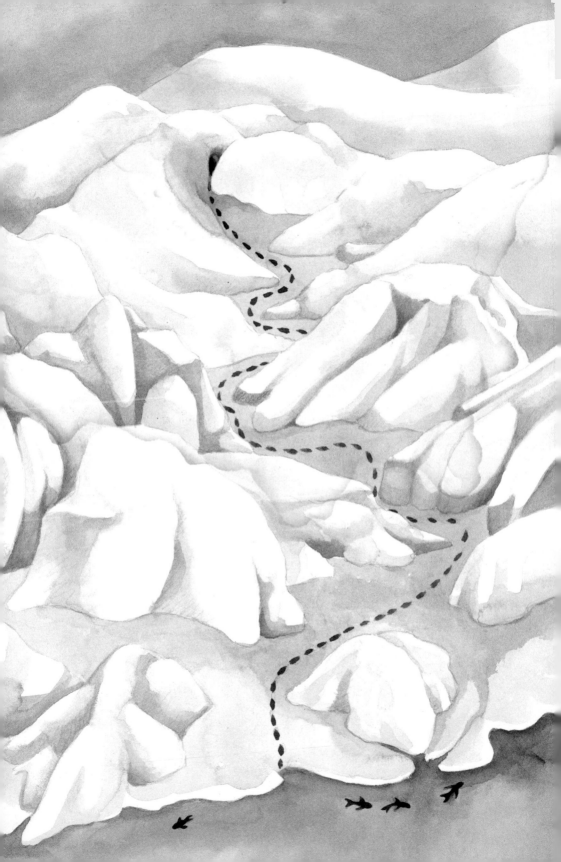

Every few hours she stops

to feed her cubs

and let them rest.

Sometimes one cub

gets to ride on her back.

At last they reach the coast.

The cubs lie quietly on the ice.

Their mother catches a big seal.

After she eats,

she brings seal meat to her cubs.

The cubs live with their mother
for two years.
After that, she leaves them.
She is ready to mate again
and have more babies.

And her cubs are ready

to live on their own.

They have only one enemy—

people.

In the past,

polar bears were hunted

for their meat and for their fur.

In more recent times,

hunters went after them for sport.

Now laws limit hunting.

Today the number

of polar bears is around 25,000.

This does not mean
polar bears are safe.
In the Arctic,
there is a lot of oil
underground.
Offshore oil rigs
can pollute the sea.

This harms polar bears
and the animals they hunt.
But perhaps the greatest danger
to polar bears comes
from global warming.
Global warming means
that the average temperature
of the Earth is rising.

Most scientists think
our modern way of life
has caused global warming.
There are too many cars
on the road.

We use too much electricity.

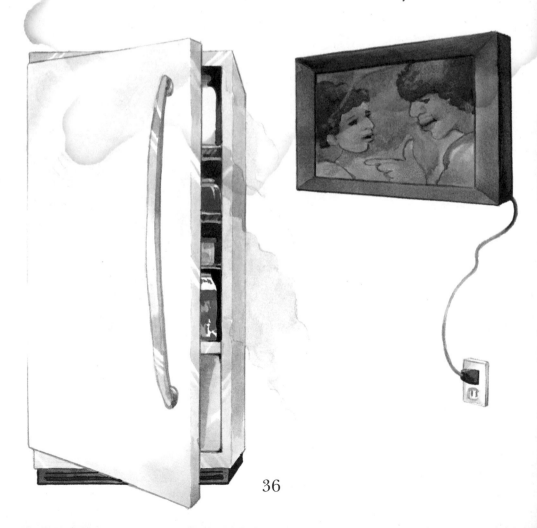

We have chopped down forests
for farming and housing.

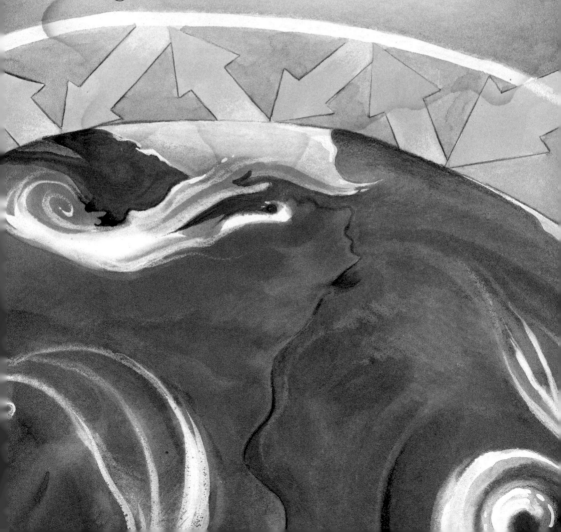

All of this sends a lot of carbon dioxide
and certain other gases into the
atmosphere.

As a group, these gases are called
greenhouse gases.

They act like the glass walls
of a greenhouse.

They hold in heat.

Our planet needs a layer
of greenhouse gases.

Without it,

Earth would be as cold as Mars.

No animals or plants

could live on Earth.

But for the past one hundred years,

we've been releasing

so much of these gases

into the atmosphere.

The layer has grown too thick.

What is the danger for
polar bears?
They hunt on the ice.
But ice in the Arctic Ocean
is melting earlier each year.
So the bears' hunting season is shorter.
Some aren't getting enough food.

Once the ice melts,

the seals swim out to sea.

It's hard to catch them there.

Sometimes the polar bears

have to swim out too far.

Some drown.

When polar bears return to land,
there is little food for them.
They must feed on fish, dead birds,
and even berries and grass.

They also look for food
in new places.
This can mean going
near people's homes.
That is dangerous for polar bears
and people!

It is not too late to stop global warming.

But everyone must help.

How?

We must use less fuel.

We should walk or ride bikes

instead of driving cars.

We should use

less electricity in our homes.

Turn off lights

before you go outside.

Or read a book

instead of watching TV!

Trees take in carbon dioxide,
one of the main greenhouse gases.
So planting more trees helps.

Our planet doesn't belong just to us.

It belongs to all creatures

living on it.

It is their home as much as ours.